The Song of
the Crocus Fairy

Crocus of yellow, new and gay;
Mauve and purple, in brave array;
        Crocus white
        Like a cup of light,—
Hundreds of them are smiling up,
Each with a flame in its shining cup,
By the touch of the warm and welcome sun
Opened suddenly. Spring's begun!
Dance then, fairies, for joy, and sing
The song of the coming again of Spring.

FLOWER
FAIRIES
OF THE
SPRING

❖

SPRING

CICELY MARY BARKER

TED SMART

Spring Magic

The World is very old;
But year by year
It groweth new again
When buds appear.

The World is very old,
And sometimes sad;
But when the daisies come
The World is glad.

The World is very old;
But every Spring
It groweth young again,
And fairies sing.

The Song of
the Colt's-Foot Fairy

The winds of March are keen and cold;
I fear them not, for I am bold.

I wait not for my leaves to grow;
They follow after: they are slow.

My yellow blooms are brave and bright;
I greet the Spring with all my might.

The
Colt's foot
Fairy.

The
Celandine
Fairy.

The Song of
the Celandine Fairy

Before the hawthorn leaves unfold,
Or buttercups put forth their gold,
By every sunny footpath shine
The stars of Lesser Celandine.

The
Willow-Catkin
Fairy.

G
M
B.

The Song of the Willow-Catkin Fairy

The people call me Palm, they do;
They call me Pussy-willow too.
And when I'm full in bloom, the bees
Come humming round my yellow trees.

The people trample round about
And spoil the little trees, and shout;
My shiny twigs are thin and brown:
The people pull and break them down.

To keep a Holy Feast, they say,
They take my pretty boughs away.
I should be glad—I should not mind—
If only people weren't unkind.

Oh, you may pick a piece, you may
(So dear and silky, soft and grey);
But if you're rough and greedy, why
You'll make the little fairies cry.

(This catkin is the flower of the Sallow Willow.)

THE SONG OF
THE WINDFLOWER FAIRY

While human-folk slumber,
   The fairies espy
Stars without number
   Sprinkling the sky.

The Winter's long sleeping,
   Like night-time, is done;
But day-stars are leaping
   To welcome the sun.

Star-like they sprinkle
   The wildwood with light;
Countless they twinkle—
   The Windflowers white!

("Windflower" is another name for
Wood Anemone.)

The
Wind
-Flower
Fairy.

The Song of the Daisy Fairy

Come to me and play with me,
   I'm the babies' flower;
Make a necklace gay with me,
Spend the whole long day with me,
   Till the sunset hour.

I must say Good-night, you know,
   Till tomorrow's playtime;
Close my petals tight, you know,
Shut the red and white, you know,
   Sleeping till the daytime.

The
Daisy
Fairy.

The
Dandelion
Fairy.

The Song of
the Dandelion Fairy

Here's the Dandelion's rhyme:
    See my leaves with tooth-like edges;
Blow my clocks to tell the time;
    See me flaunting by the hedges,
In the meadow, in the lane,
    Gay and naughty in the garden;
Pull me up—I grow again,
    Asking neither leave nor pardon.
Sillies, what are you about
    With your spades and hoes of iron?
You can never drive me out—
    Me, the dauntless Dandelion!

The Song of
the Daffodil Fairy

I'm everyone's darling: the blackbird and
    starling
Are shouting about me from blossoming
    boughs;
For I, the Lent Lily, the Daffy-down-dilly,
Have heard through the country the call to
    arouse.
The orchards are ringing with voices
    a-singing
The praise of my petticoat, praise of my
    gown;
The children are playing, and hark! they are
    saying
That Daffy-down-dilly is come up to town!

The
Daffodil
Fairy.

The
Dog~Violet
Fairy.

CMB.

The Song of
the Dog-Violet Fairy

The wren and robin hop around;
   The Primrose-maids my neighbours be;
The sun has warmed the mossy ground;
Where Spring has come, I too am found:
   The Cuckoo's call has wakened me!

The Song of
the Primrose Fairy

The Primrose opens wide in spring;
   Her scent is sweet and good:
It smells of every happy thing
   In sunny lane and wood.
I have not half the skill to sing
   And praise her as I should.

She's dear to folk throughout the land;
   In her is nothing mean:
She freely spreads on every hand
   Her petals pale and clean.
And though she's neither proud nor grand,
   She is the Country Queen.

The
Primrose
Fairy.

The Song of
the Lady's-Smock Fairy

Where the grass is damp and green,
Where the shallow streams are flowing,
Where the cowslip buds are showing,
    I am seen.

Dainty as a fairy's frock,
White or mauve, of elfin sewing,
'Tis the meadow-maiden growing—
    Lady's-smock.

The Song of the Larch Fairy

Sing a song of Larch trees
    Loved by fairy-folk;
Dark stands the pinewood,
    Bare stands the oak,
But the Larch is dressed and trimmed
    Fit for fairy-folk!

Sing a song of Larch trees,
    Sprays that swing aloft,
Pink tufts, and tassels
    Grass-green and soft:
All to please the little elves
    Singing songs aloft!

THE SONG OF
THE BLUEBELL FAIRY

My hundred thousand bells of blue,
  The splendour of the Spring,
They carpet all the woods anew
With royalty of sapphire hue;
The Primrose is the Queen, 'tis true.
    But surely I am King!
      Ah yes,
    The peerless Woodland King!

Loud, loud the thrushes sing their song;
  The bluebell woods are wide;
My stems are tall and straight and strong;
From ugly streets the children throng,
They gather armfuls, great and long,
    Then home they troop in pride—
      Ah yes,
    With laughter and with pride!

(This is the Wild Hyacinth. The Bluebell of Scotland
is the Harebell.)

The Song of
the Stitchwort Fairy

I am brittle-stemmed and slender,
But the grass is my defender.

On the banks where grass is long,
I can stand erect and strong.

All my mass of starry faces
Looking up from wayside places,

From the thick and tangled grass,
Gives you greeting as you pass.

(A prettier name for Stitchwort is
Starwort, but it is not so often used.)

The
Stitchwort
Fairy.

The Song of the Wood-Sorrel Fairy

In the wood the trees are tall,
   Up and up they tower;
You and I are very small—
   Fairy-child and flower.

Bracken stalks are shooting high,
   Far and far above us;
We are little, you and I,
   But the fairies love us.

The
Wood Sorrel
Fairy.

The
Speedwell
Fairy

The Song of the Speedwell Fairy

Clear blue are the skies;
    My petals are blue;
    As beautiful, too,
As bluest of eyes.

The heavens are high:
    By the field-path I grow
    Where wayfarers go,
And "Good speed," say I;

"See, here is a prize
    Of wonderful worth:
    A weed of the earth,
As blue as the skies!"

(There are many kinds of
Speedwell: this is the Germander.)

The Song of the Lords-and-Ladies Fairy

Here's the song of Lords-and-Ladies
   (in the damp and shade he grows):
I have neither bells nor petals,
   like the foxglove or the rose.
Through the length and breadth of England,
   many flowers you may see—
Petals, bells, and cups in plenty—
   but there's no one else like me.

In the hot-house dwells my kinsman,
   Arum-lily, white and fine;
I am not so tall and stately,
   but the quaintest hood is mine;
And my glossy leaves are handsome;
   I've a spike to make you stare;
And my berries are a glory in September.
   (BUT BEWARE!)

(The Wild Arum has other names beside
Lords-and-/Ladies, such as Cuckoo-pint and
Jack-in-the-Pulpit.)

The
Lords-and-Ladies
Fairy.

The
Cowslip
Fairy.

THE SONG OF
THE COWSLIP FAIRY

The land is full of happy birds
And flocks of sheep and grazing herds.

I hear the songs of larks that fly
Above me in the breezy sky.

I hear the little lambkins bleat;
My honey-scent is rich and sweet.

Beneath the sun I dance and play
In April and in merry May.

The grass is green as green can be;
The children shout at sight of me.

The Song of the Heart's-Ease Fairy

Like the richest velvet
　　(I've heard the fairies tell)
Grow the handsome pansies
　　within the garden wall;
When you praise their beauty,
　　remember me as well—
Think of little Heart's-ease,
　　the brother of them all!

Come away and seek me
　　when the year is young,
Through the open ploughlands
　　beyond the garden wall;
Many names are pretty
　　and many songs are sung:
Mine—because I'm Heart's-ease—
　　are prettiest of all!

(An old lady says that when she was a little
girl the children's name for the Heart's-ease
or Wild Pansy was Jump-up-and-kiss-me!)

The
Heart'sease
Fairy.

The Song of
the May Fairy

My buds, they cluster small and green;
  The sunshine gaineth heat:
Soon shall the hawthorn tree be clothed
  As with a snowy sheet.

O magic sight, the hedge is white,
  My scent is very sweet;
And lo, where I am come indeed,
  The Spring and Summer meet.

The
May
Fairy.

*The reproductions in this book have been made using the most modern electronic
scanning methods. The original watercolours have been lost so we have used
a first edition to reproduce these pictures.*

FREDERICK WARNE

Published by the Penguin Group
27 Wrights Lane, London W8 5TZ, England
Penguin Putnam Inc, 375 Hudson Street, New York, N.Y. 10014, USA
Penguin Books Australia Ltd, Ringwood, Victoria, Australia
Penguin Books Canada Ltd, 10 Alcorn Avenue, Toronto, Ontario, Canada M4V 3B2
Penguin Books (NZ) Ltd, 182-190 Wairau Road, Auckland 10, New Zealand

Penguin Books Ltd, Registered Offices: Harmondsworth, Middlesex, England

First published 1923
Edition with new reproductions first published 1990
This edition first published 1999

1 3 5 7 9 10 8 6 4 2

ISBN 0 7232 4561 4

Printed in Dubai by Oriental Press